THE CAPTAIN AND THE LADY

THE TRENGROUSE BALL

BOOK ONE

ELIZABETH LEYDIN

IMPROBABLE FICTIONS

ISBN 978-1-7635241-3-2

Improbable Fictions
PO Box 283
Annandale NSW 2038
Australia
contact@improbablefictions.com

THE TRENGROUSE BALL

The Trengrouse Ball…one magic night in a Cornish summer. Music, dancing, flirting and laughter. And deception, abduction, love and loss. New attractions, new hopes, and old flames rekindled. For some, a culmination. For others, a new beginning.

The Trengrouse Ball series follows the lives and loves of the Trengrouse family: eight grown children of the Earl of Trengrouse, each of whom is searching for the life they need; each battling their own fears but hoping for happy ever after.

After the Trengrouse Ball, their lives will never be the same again…

CHAPTER 1

AUGUST 1815

He was coming. Beatrice smoothed her skirt down and pushed a hairpin more firmly into place. A deep breath, and she moved to the gate.

Captain Trengrouse surged up the road from the cove, thumping his wooden crutches into the ground at each step, his buff jacket straining over his arms. His left breeches leg flapped below his knee at each step. She should really offer to sew it up for him; the pin he used to secure it came out so often, and she knew he hated that.

Perhaps he felt it drew more attention to his missing leg.

How could she phrase this? She had planned the conversation over and over, but still, there were no words which felt anywhere near acceptable.

He neared the gate, and she pulled it open. His face was flushed from the climb up the road; his black hair still wet from his daily swim. So handsome. She *tried* not to notice, but he was impossible to ignore. She had even had a most improper dream about him.

"Thank you." He swung in and began to head for the house. She had to say something *now*.

"Captain."

He turned back, attentive good manners on show.

"Lady Beatrice? I'm at your service."

"If you'd come and sit with me a moment?"

"Of course."

They went to sit in the bower – a wooden

seat under an arch of roses at the side of the yard. The heavy scent enveloped them. It was a romantic spot, and she wished fervently that they were there for romance instead of-

"Captain." Another deep breath. "When your mother suggested that you come to stay with us, naturally we were delighted…" At least her *mother* had been delighted. She had been… wary.

"It was very kind of your mother to invite me." Oh, that voice. So smooth and deep, like chocolate. *Breathe, Beatrice.*

"Yes." She met his eyes, knowing that her own showed her worry. For the first time, because a lady never revealed any concern in public. "Captain, we simply can't afford you."

He blinked and sat back. "I don't-"

"My mother is on a very small jointure. My inheritance from my grandmother is also small. We live…simply."

Frowning, he pushed his crutches to the side as if to concentrate better. "Your mother is the Dowager Countess of Mannering!"

"Yes." Beatrice bent her head, feeling the embarrassed blush rising on her cheeks. How mortifying this was. "My mother's dowage is based on her dowry, which was… small." Her parents had married for love; wonderful, except where finances were concerned.

"Your father must have made provision."

She shook her head.

"My father knew that my brother would take care of Mama." And so he would have. Just as he would have provided her with a decent dowry. But the carriage accident had taken both father and brother in one fell swoop.

"But the current Earl…"

"The current Earl is my father's cousin. He had no finances of his own, and he has five daughters." The mealy-mouthed, tight-fisted old, old *bastard*. He had virtually thrown them out. If Mama's godmother hadn't left her this house, they would be homeless.

Captain Trengrouse drew in a deep

breath and sat right back. "So I am a drain on your resources."

Her mother insisted that a man recovering from an almost-deadly wound needed meat. Every day. Before he had come, they had existed on fish from local fishermen and home-grown vegetables. And even then, they'd barely got by.

"I'm sorry-"

Holding up a hand, he half-laughed. There was a bitter note to it. "There is a simple solution, Lady Beatrice. I shall pay for my lodgings."

It was like being slapped. She reared back in affront. How dare he! Offer her money as though she were a common innkeeper!

Perhaps he saw that in her face. He leaned forwards, speaking earnestly. "I meant no offense, my lady. But..." His hand touched his left knee. "I've improved so much since being here. My doctor was right – sea bathing *is* a good cure for my...for me."

Now it was his turn to colour with embarrassment. Mortifying for him, too, to have to admit his weakness. The poor man. If it was doing him good to live quietly with them here in Semper House, to bathe every morning in the sea, to sit each night and read in their parlour while her mother embroidered and she played her pianoforte...

She sighed. "Very well, Captain. But I have no idea what I should ask of you."

He grinned. The sudden change in his face was startling. She'd never seen any sign of humour before; he had been uniformly grim and dour. It transformed him. She couldn't resist smiling in return, and her heart beat faster. Ridiculous.

"When I stayed at the Golden Hind in Portsmouth, it cost me eight pounds a week, and the food is definitely better here. Not to mention the company. Ten, perhaps?"

Ten pounds! There had been a time in her life when ten pounds meant nothing. A new fan. An embroidered petticoat. Now it meant so much. *Be calm. Act like a lady.*

"Thank you, Captain. Perhaps..." Could she bear him handing money over to her?

She felt sick at the thought. "Perhaps you could give that to Mrs Marrak."

His grin shifted into an understanding smile. "Of course. Thank you." Hesitating, he cleared his throat. "It means a great deal to me, Lady Beatrice. I'm genuinely in your debt."

Concentrate on that. Do not, at any point, consider that you're now in Trade.

"And perhaps we don't need to mention this to my mother…? Or to yours?"

He actually had the gall to laugh! And then waved his hand. "Don't worry, Lady Beatrice. I'd never tell either of them!"

Her mother and the Countess of St Aubin were peas in a pod, and had been friends since girlhood.

"Including not telling your mother our… circumstances."

He looked surprised. She had been, too, when she'd found out that her mother hadn't revealed their situation to her oldest friend.

"I couldn't *bear* that people knew!" Tears had flowed down her mother's face, a thing she'd only ever seen once before, when their beloveds had died. "I couldn't *bear* it, Beatrice!" So she had promised not to tell anyone of their acquaintance. She hoped telling the captain didn't break that promise.

"Certainly." The captain's voice was soft, and understanding.

"Well then." Beatrice rose to her feet, trying to stiffen knees which were shaky with relief. "We can go on as before."

He hoisted himself upright, using one crutch for balance. "Yes," he said, an odd dry note in his voice. "Just as before."

CHAPTER 2

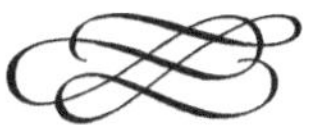

That poor girl!

He hadn't had any idea things were so bad. Petroc stumped up the stairs, his crutches in his right hand. He gripped the handrail firmly with his left and hoisted himself up, using the railing as a crutch. It was laborious, but safer than trying to go up using the crutches themselves, as he'd discovered soon after his return to England, when he'd tumbled down a staircase at the inn.

Fortunately, everyone had assumed he was drunk.

He wished he had been, but on doctor's orders he'd had no more than a glassful of wine with dinner. And not even that since he'd come to Swain Cove, since the ladies didn't drink wine with their meals.

Of course! He'd thought they were on some reducing diet, but the truth was they couldn't *afford* wine. And yet the dowager had offered him some damn fine brandy on his first night.

It *was* Cornwall. Smugglers galore. Grinning to himself, he made it to the top of the stairs and headed for his room. He collapsed into the chair and stared at the strangely naked bed. Where had the eiderdown gone?

Some household matter, probably. Perhaps they were airing it. It was a lovely day. He'd enjoyed his swim, rather than endured it as he had the first few weeks.

Lord, he'd been eating the family out of house and home for three weeks now! He'd better hand over the readies to Mrs Marrak straight away. And back pay it, too. He had some money tucked away.

His mother could *not* be aware of how things stood here, or she'd have had the two of them living at Trengrouse Hall. Too late now to take back his promise; a shame. She definitely wouldn't have sent him here to convalesce if she'd known.

He'd been so grateful for the respite, and it had seemed quite natural, to go and stay with his mother's best friend, even though he hadn't known the family that well, since they mingled mostly in London and he'd been serving in Portugal and then France.

He'd assumed this was a summer cottage, but it must be their year-long home. It would seem tiny to Beatrice, after the mansion she'd grown up in. But it had been a welcome retreat to him.

Trengrouse Hall was also big, but it held a lot of people. His parents and six unmarried siblings, his eldest brother and wife, servants, the steward, and an unceasing progression of guests – either social or business. The tin mines a few miles from the house were a family concern, and, unlike most aristocrats, his family had always had a few fingers in trade pies.

There had been no peace there. Getting away to the beach had been impossible without a retinue of children, nannies and grooms. And the beach was too far to walk. He'd had to drive his curricle, which hurt his leg damnably whenever they went over a bump.

Here…he hopped to the window. Semper House was on the hill above the cove, and looked down over the roofs of the village to the inlet and, to the left, the sea. A quiet, small place with a sandy bay along the coast where he could swim undisturbed each morning. And then back to the house, to rest for a while (more doctor's orders), and then to sit in the garden, and quietly admire Lady Beatrice as she tended the plants there, and another walk later.

She had been kind to him, but only with the kindness due a guest, and none extra because of his leg. In fact, now he thought about it, she had never mentioned or even *looked* at his leg the whole time he'd been here. Her quiet, distant courtesy had been a blessing.

He would be fitted with a wooden half-leg and foot when he went up to London to resign his commission in a few weeks, but he was determined to be otherwise as fit as any man there when he swung in. He might be a cripple, but he wouldn't be pitiful.

By God, he wouldn't!

Lady Beatrice hadn't meant anything by her, "We can go on as before," but it had cut him deep. There was no going on as before for him. No more Army. No more serving his country.

What good was he to anyone now? His father had been clear enough. "I can always use a good man in the office," he'd said. In the office.

The very thought stifled him, and he pulled the damp cotton scarf from around his neck. He used it to wipe himself down after his swim, but it also disguised the fact he had no collar or neckcloth on.

Mrs Marrak had left him warm water, as always, so he stripped and washed the salt from his skin, before dressing as a gentleman and an officer again. He went to the window as he did up the buttons on his waistcoat. His uniform was damned hot. Could he leave the jacket off if he went out again? Technically, he could wear mufti while he was on sick leave, but some part of him wanted to sport that scarlet coat as much as he could. While he could.

Damn it, he was acting like a maudlin fool!

Lady Beatrice left through the front gate and went off downhill. Such a fine young woman. He had thought her a little subdued for true beauty, a little flat, but now that he knew what she was dealing with – by Jove, she was a trooper! Shouldering all the responsibility for this place, for her mother…It was a true shame he'd promised not to tell his mother about their situation, because she'd make a fine wife for Felix. There were of an age, a few years younger than he, and

Felix had always been shy with girls. Having Beatrice to stay would be the very thing to get him out of his shell.

And that would solve everything.

Lying down on the bed for the hour his doctor insisted on, he ignored the strange ache in his lower chest. Overdone it a bit, perhaps, with the swim. It wasn't that he envied Felix, with his life still ahead of him and no…no *impediments* to marriage.

Surely not.

CHAPTER 3

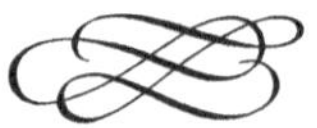

"You can't tell anyone!" Beatrice frowned at Charity Penhaligon.

"Oh, of course not!" Charity's clever hazel eyes narrowed shrewdly. "You must have been *mortified*."

It was such a relief to pour it all out to Charity. She was the only bright spot in the dismal life they were living. Intelligent, gentle in birth and quick in understanding, she was the first true friend Beatrice had ever had.

It turned out that meeting other young women at balls and picnics allowed less true conversation than, as they were doing now, making up a large quantity of soup for distribution to the poor of the parish. The August heat made the kitchen hot and humid, but Beatrice wouldn't be here for the actual cooking – she was chopping carrots and turnips in preparation.

Beatrice laughed, and Charity looked up from cutting bacon off a fletch.

"What's so funny?"

"I was just imagining the looks on the faces of my fellow debutantes if they saw me doing this!"

Charity laughed too. "God's work, Bea. They should be doing the same." Charity was the vicar's daughter. Doing God's work came easily to her.

"I have to find a way to get more income." Beatrice dumped a bowlful of carrots into the cast-iron cauldron and reached for more.

"There's the traditional way…" Marriage. The only acceptable way for a lady to "acquire" income.

"Without a dowry?"

Charity sighed. "You'll have to fall in love, as I did."

"And I have so much choice!"

"God will find a way – and at least I'll have you to keep me company until Hector comes back from London. We should hold a party, and have you meet the local possibilities, such as they are."

Her husband, Hector Penhaligon, had been appointed to an attaché's position in Rome, and was being "brought up to snuff" in London. He'd suggested Charity come back for a last visit with her mother before they sailed, and she'd gladly escaped the London August heat. It was lovely to have her back, even for a couple of weeks. And she was so *practical* about things like love.

"I suppose we could…" she said. Local possibilities. That sounded so *dire*. As though there would be only mushrooms, boys, and aged roués to choose from.

But what was she prepared to do to save her mother from poverty?

It was her duty. And what she'd been raised for, after all.

As she walked home, it was as though there were two of her. One was excited by the thought of music and dancing, and talking to someone new, and perhaps finding love. The other was revolted by the idea of selling herself off to some stranger for the sake of a little security. Because she knew who would marry an impoverished daughter of the nobility: a jumped-up Cit who wanted to bag a titled wife.

Neither side would give up.

Could she have the enjoyment, the music and the dancing, without the "arrangement"? the giddy side wondered. *You're being too nice in your requirements*, the sensible part said. *You're virtually in trade yourself, so you can't afford to be picky.*

That was a depressing thought. She went inside and through to the kitchen, where Mrs Marrak met her with a smile.

"Captain came to see me," she said.

"No mention of this to my mother."

"Oh, no! No call t'bother m'lady. I've put the readies in the desk drawer, and kept some to pay the grocer and the butcher."

Beatrice smiled her thanks. Mrs Marrak and her husband had come with the house. A sturdy dark-haired Cornishwoman, she had looked after the dowager's godmother for more than twenty years. It wouldn't have been surprising if she'd resented the new owners, but it wasn't so.

"For your mother, God bless her, was always so kind to Lady Gwen," she'd said on their first day. "Paid for her winter wood, every year, and come to see her regular. And frankly, milady, we're just as pleased not to have to find another position at our time of life."

Thank God for that. Although, only God knew where the winter wood would come from this year. She would have to budget for that. How much did wood cost? She had no idea. The wood at Mannering had come from their own coppices.

Her mother drifted to the door.

"Beatrice! What are you doing in the kitchen?"

"Just giving Mrs Marrak some instructions, Mama." Beatrice made an apologetic face at Mrs Marrak and guided her mother back to the drawing room – such as it was. A ground floor chamber, it was scarcely big enough for its two sofas and the armchair which was her mother's particular place.

"One should not go to the kitchen to give instructions, Beatrice. One should summon the servant to one."

"Mrs Marrak has too much to do, Mama, to be running after me all day."

Her mother smiled indulgently. They had been here fourteen months, and her father and brother had been dead for more than a year, and in all that time her mother had not complained once, nor even raised a sigh.

Beatrice would not have blamed her if she

had. She had gone from being the mistress of a country mansion, a London townhouse, a Bath house for summer…wanting for nothing, never thinking about pounds, let alone pence.

If you needed a ball for three hundred people planned and executed to the highest possible Society standard, her mother would cope admirably. But making sure they had enough flour for the daily baking? It was so far outside her experience as to be impossible for her.

It hadn't been easy for Bea to adjust, but she, at least, was not unlearning a lifetime of how to live. She missed her old home with a deep, yearning ache, but the day to day necessities of life here gave her something to *do*. The hours passed so slowly otherwise. And she wasn't her mother, to be able to give her full attention to embroidery.

"Come, Mama, the eiderdown needs mending."

"Of course." Her mother settled in her chair, her sewing box next to her, and began to darn the worn-through eiderdown from the captain's room. She had never complained. *Never.* Beatrice wouldn't either.

They were lucky to have this house, she told herself fiercely. Lucky to have enough to live on, even if it wasn't much. And perhaps, if she went to the Assemblies, she would be lucky enough to find someone to love who would love her.

An assessment of her clothes was in order. Surely, as Charity had said, they could freshen up her ball gowns? After all, this wasn't London.

She ignored the piercing of her heart that thought caused. The cascade of memories of London seasons, before her family had been destroyed. She had had suitors, then, with the promise of a generous dowry implied. Few had kept calling once their circumstances were known; and those few hadn't followed her to Cornwall. She couldn't blame them.

But she felt so *alone*. There was no one to rely on any more. Mama was wonderful, but she managed nothing. There was no one to take any responsibility. Only her.

Blinking back tears, she went out into the garden to gather vegetables for the evening meal. Marrak had promised there would be new potatoes and asparagus, and she could pick some peas and pull a couple of young carrots.

Like a peasant, came a voice in her mind, unpleasantly like her grandmother's, who had been a stickler for propriety and "standards".

Few peasants were this well fed, she reminded herself. But when she saw the dirt under her nails from pulling the carrots, she wondered if anyone, anywhere, would look at her and see a lady.

CHAPTER 4

A bustle at the gate made Beatrice look out the window, where she had sat to catch the last of the light for her sewing.

The captain looked up too. "Horses," he said. "Two of them."

"Hoy the house!" came from outside their gate.

"Who could that be?" Her mother sat a little straighter, her mouth tight. Beatrice and the captain went to the front door together, which Mrs Marrak was already opening.

At their gate, a man held two horses. She knew them all.

"Bob!" Beatrice raced out, calling for Marrak. "Bob, what are you doing here?"

"Sent down by his lordship, Miss Bea." He grinned, his missing front tooth giving him the inimitable smile she'd known since she was born. He jerked his head at the chestnut he had on a leading string, though it was saddled.

Rubicon.

"Ruby? What on earth?"

The horse, hearing her voice, shouldered his way around the bay – surely that was Blaze – to nose at her cheek.

"Ruby." She didn't even have a carrot, let alone a sugar cube, but it didn't matter. Ruby blew gently into her face and Beatrice buried her head in the stallion's neck to hide her tears.

Marrak came around the side of the house and reached them.

"Kin put 'em in the old barn, miss, if'n you please."

Beatrice drew a long breath and pulled away from the horse, who snuffled after her. "Oh, yes, that would be fine, Marrak. You might need to get some straw in?"

"Got some for bedding down the sparagus, miss, just the other day. Always buy it in summer; by the time ye need it, price's sky high."

She couldn't follow that, but it was fine.

"And ask Mrs Marrak for some oats."

"Yes'm." He took the horses and led them away, but Beatrice put a hand out when Bob would have followed. "Bob, why are you here?"

Bob grinned widely again. "An'nt no one who can ride 'im, Miss, since you left. And the Earl, he said that he'd have no animal eating his head off who couldn't be used, an he wanted to put him down. But Reeve said animal belonged t'you, so he said, 'Then she can have the stabling of him!' juss like that, miss. So here I am."

Ruby was hers again!

"I see. Well, go along with Marrak and he'll see you settled. Thank you, Bob."

Bob touched his hand to his cap and went off.

She'd forgotten the captain was behind her. "So he's just dumped this animal on you, knowing you can't afford to keep it? Quite a piece of work, this new earl."

Her momentary elation dropped away. Of course they couldn't afford a horse. That was why she'd left him behind in the first place.

"I suppose we can...I can...I'll have to sell him – but at least I'll get some riding in first!"

There had been bundles on Ruby's back. His tack, presumably. Bob would have seen to that. For summer, at least, he could graze in the field by the old barn. She'd been thinking about getting a cow with her quarterly allowance, but there wasn't feed for three animals there, so that would have to wait.

"I envy you." The captain's voice was low;

she wasn't sure he'd meant her to hear. Kindest to ignore it.

"I'll just go around to the barn," she said. She couldn't possibly leave Ruby there without brushing him down herself, and checking the two horses were well stabled.

"May I come?" he asked, quite formally. She smiled at him. The two of them were both riders, and both deprived of riding. If he wanted to rub salt in that wound, that was his prerogative.

"Of course, captain."

They walked around to the barn in companionable silence.

LADY BEATRICE'S barn was an old building, not falling down but with shingles missing and the odd hole in the wall.

He'd not gone in there before – the doors had always been closed and he hadn't been sure of his ability to pull one open without toppling over. It was a huge space, the back half left clear for hay storage, the near half divided into solid horse stalls, panelled in oak up to his chest and then slatted above, so the horses could be inspected without opening the stall door.

"These are stallion stalls!"

"That's right," Marrak said. "Lady Gwen's husband's father, he was a horse trader. Never bred much, but he dickered for 'em in Newmarket and then sold 'em off down this way. Some good racing round here."

"Flat racing?" Lady Beatrice asked.

Marrak coughed and spat. "Nah then, that's not a race for a man. Steeple chase, cross country, that's our game."

Petroc couldn't help grinning. "And good fun it is."

"'Tis indeed."

"Miss Bea is the one for cross country," Bob came out of the stall where he'd put the chestnut. "Right from when she was a young thing, she'd just take off and let the horse follow his head, and turn around when she got hungry. The grooms couldn't keep up with her."

"No tales out of school," Lady Beatrice said, smiling. She inspected the chestnut's stall and nodded approval, then produced a carrot she'd pulled from the garden on their way through. The other horse whinnied. "Yes, and one for you too, girl." She fed the bay mare through the slats and scratched her under the chin.

Her ease with the horses was astonishing. Where was the correct and slightly distant Lady Beatrice he'd come to know?

As though she felt him looking, she cast a glance towards him and moved back from the horses, once more assuming her ladylike demeanour. A twinge of something very like regret went through him.

"So Ruby is yours? And this one?" He nodded towards the bay.

"Blaze? She was my mother's mount, on the few occasions Mama rode."

A lady's horse? The groom, Bob, had ridden him with just a blanket, which must have been deuced uncomfortable.

"No saddle?" Petroc raised an eyebrow at Bob.

"None the earl would lend me. Blaze was trained to side saddle, not astride, for her ladyship. I've brought that, but it was easier for me without. She's used to me riding her up to the stables like this." Of course. A faint, elusive hope that he might be able to try riding himself vanished. A sidesaddle horse wasn't going to take easily to a man's saddle.

Bob came out of the stall and hesitated, looking at the ground.

"I'm just as pleased he didn't lend me a saddle, begging your pardon, Miss Bea. Means I don't have to go back."

"You're leaving Mannering Hall?"

Shuffling his feet a little, Bob nodded. "Not the first, either, miss. There's a few of us don't like the way the new earl is handing things."

"Miss Bea" put a hand up. "I can't listen to gossip about my cousin, Bob."

"No, miss. But...if you had a place for me here..."

Her eyes filled with compassion and—was that shame?

"I'm sorry, Bob, we won't be keeping the horses on-"

Petroc cut in. "I can offer you employment." He spoke impulsively, but it was true. Without his batman, who'd been killed at Waterloo, his clothes and especially his one uniform boot were becoming scruffy.

This Bob wasn't a valet, obviously, but he was a good man and there was something solid and trustworthy about him. Ten years as an officer had given him a good eye for a decent man.

"Captain, are you sure?" Lady Beatrice's voice was one he'd never heard from her. Higher, younger – sweeter. It warmed him, and so did the hope in her eyes.

"If Bob is. I knew I'd have to replace my batman sooner or later. Look after my clothes, shine my boots."

Bob grinned. "Ay, Cap'n, I can do that. Not so good at the fancy stuff, though."

Petroc twisted his mouth awry in a half-smile. "Do I look as though I'm fancy?"

Considering him with a serious air, Bob shook his head. "You look like a right 'un."

Odd, how that brief assessment settled something in him. Apart from anything else, it would be good to have another man around. He'd been spending all his time with women; so odd after years of Army life.

"Right, then, I'll pay you whatever you were getting from the Earl, plus your keep."

"Thankee, sir. And I can still look after the ladies' mounts?"

"As long as we're here, certainly."

Beatrice flashed him a grateful smile, and then turned to Bob.

"We'll sort out a bed for you in one of the attic rooms, then. Will Ruby be up to taking me out tomorrow?"

"Oh, certain sure, miss. Took 'em in easy stages, like."

"Excellent." She looked Bob dead in the eye. "Did you tell the earl you were leaving permanently?"

"Oh, no, miss! He'd never have let me bring the two nags down to you if'n he'd known that."

"I'll write to him then."

She nodded to them both and went back to the house.

"I could write for you, if you preferred," Petroc offered.

"Leave it to Miss Bea," Bob said. "There's nothing she can't do."

Stumping back up the path, Petroc wondered about that. Nothing she can't do. She'd certainly adapted to penury with grace and dignity, but perhaps that dignity was a way of holding on to her...her poise? Her own self-respect? She'd been a different woman with those horses.

And tomorrow she'd ride.

Goddamn it. He wished he could adapt to being a cripple as well as she had adapted to poverty.

CHAPTER 5

Oh, to be back riding! And on not just any horse, but her own Rubicon.

Beatrice patted his neck and walked him through the farm gate at the back of their field, closing it again behind her with her riding crop. A manoeuvre it had taken hours of practice to perfect. Ruby didn't like gates.

But now they were free to ride the trail through the woods at a steady canter. She leaned forward just a little, clicked her tongue, and they were off.

There was nothing like this. Wind in her

hair, Ruby's strong legs drumming on the ground, no one watching her, no one to be ladylike or composed or well mannered for…no one to take care of.

Just her and Ruby and the beautiful summer day, so hot she'd wanted to take off her riding jacket as soon as she'd put it on. She hadn't, of course. Not ladylike. But here, in the dappled shade of beech and hazel… who would care? She reined Ruby in and shrugged out of her jacket, tucking it in front of her, partly under the second saddle bow which held her right knee steady. She could use some extra padding there; it had been so long, she'd lost all the right muscles to keep her legs strong, and her knee kept bumping against it.

No matter. She'd get those muscles back now.

But as she set off again along the track, her elation seeped away. What was the point of getting fit again if she had no horse? She couldn't afford *not* to sell Ruby. A well trained lady's hunter would pay the winter wood bill for quite a few years.

In fact, it would pay for a coppice, which would give them charcoal and withies and chair reeds and wicker and more. This coppice she was riding through was adjacent to their land. The farmer who owned it might be willing to sell.

Then she could come to some agreement with a woodsman where they shared the output of the wood.

There were all sorts of ways of profiting from a coppice, and the wind off the coast made it hard to grow one in this area, so the outputs were worth more than they were back at Easterlake. Behind their new house, the land dipped into a sheltered dell, where the woods thrived.

Land management. A much more fitting way to make money than renting out rooms!

Ruby's price could get them that. And Blaze's would pay for more – the cow, the cost of putting the cow to bull so they'd get a calf and milk, winter feed…so much. She was turning into one of the smallholders who had been tenants of her father. The thought put a sour taste in her mouth, but not because of snobbery. Just that her life had become so *small*. So closed in, day after day the same, day after day after day, nothing but making ends meet and worry, and the only company being Charity and her mother, and now Charity was off to Rome, a place she'd probably never see…

A gust of salty air made her realise she'd reached the edge of the small wood. Before her stretched pastureland. A little to her right, the road cut through, and on the other side of the road, sheep fields rose up to the cliffs.

Enough worrying. She would enjoy this ride to the fullest, and every ride thereafter, until she had to sell Ruby.

His afternoon walk was always hard. Petroc stumped up the hill from Semper

House in a temper – with himself, mostly, for being weak enough to find it difficult.

He'd campaigned through the Pyrenees, for God's sake! He'd climbed actual *mountains*. And here he was, almost defeated by a little Cornish hill.

Not today. Today he'd make it to the top.

The last few yards were painful, but he was heading for one particular spot – an old standing stone which had fallen sideways into the grass, and which would make a good seat where he could recover and see the view. That would be his reward. The summer hills and fields of home, the familiar blue-green of the sea.

He climbed laboriously through a stile and set off on an angle to reach the stone. Not far now.

The stone was only a few steps away when Lady Beatrice came over the brow of the hill at a canter. He was struck dumb at the sight; she rode like an Amazon, one with the horse, and her face was alight with joy.

It was like being kicked under the heart.

All his breath left his body and he stood there mumchance, like a nodcock.

She reined in as soon as she saw him, and smiled, indicating the view with a sweep of her hand.

"Isn't it beautiful?"

"Yes." He didn't look away from her. A faint pink rose in her cheeks, and he realised he was staring. It was harder than it should have been to turn away and look back at the Cove and the cliffs running down to the sea. Yes, it was beautiful on this day of scudding clouds and bright flashes of sun.

She was dismounting. He tried to get there in time to help her, but she needed no help. She swung her leg out of its holder, turned, and slid down the horse's side as if she'd done it a million times before. Perhaps she had, on those mad rides Bob had mentioned.

His leg sent a shaft of pain through him, and he bit the inside of his cheek to stop it showing. But he had to sit down.

"Do you have a moment to sit and enjoy

the view?" he asked. Such a gentleman, pretending to sit for her sake!

"Just a moment. I don't want to leave Ruby up here in the wind."

They sat side by side on the stone, Ruby's reins still in her hand. He rubbed his knee, and she followed the movement with her gaze.

"Why not ride back with me?"

That was more like being slapped in the face. "I don't ride anymore."

"You could come up behind me." Her face was carefully blank; she was making sure he didn't see the pity she no doubt felt. Being *kind*. Anger surged up. If only he could throw her pity back in her face. But a gentleman couldn't.

"Thank you, but I don't think that would work."

"Then perhaps you should take my place."

She couldn't be serious.

Lady Beatrice hesitated, but went on. "You're still recovering. There's no shame in obeying doctor's orders to be careful."

"Take your *place*?" How ridiculous he would look, riding sidesaddle! He could hear the scorn in his own voice.

She flushed, but ploughed on. "I don't see why you couldn't ride sidesaddle. It might not be *ideal*, but at least you'd be back on a horse! I- I've missed riding so much…if I were you, I'd take any possibility of getting back on a mount."

She peeped up at him. "No one's looking. You could give it a try…"

The rock was here, just the right height for a mounting block. All around them, there was just the open air, the soft sea grass, the blue sky above, and the wind, blowing the smell of salt and freedom. No one to see.

Laying a hand on his arm, Beatrice smiled mischievously up at him, and his heart kicked. "I promise not to tell."

His mouth twisted awry, but he couldn't help smiling. "On your head be it. If I fall off and break my back, I'll know who to blame."

She laughed. He'd never heard her laugh before, and it rang in him like bells, pushing him to his feet. She stood too, and brought Ruby around to stand behind the stone, ready. She whispered in Ruby's ear and the horse stood quietly.

"So, how….?"

"Up you get, and then I'll help you. Just don't put your right leg on the other side." She let down the stirrup as though she'd done it a thousand times before, once again seeming far more at ease with horses than she was in the drawing room.

He put his left foot in the stirrup and pushed up, twisting so that his right leg sat parallel to his left. It was damned uncomfortable.

Beatrice pushed at him until he was almost facing forwards. "Do you mind…?" she asked, but didn't wait for an answer before she took hold of his right leg above the knee and pushed it up until it fit in between the edge of the saddle and a kind of protrusion which stopped it going lower.

Damned uncomfortable! If women had to ride like this, they were martyrs! Ruby skittered from side to side, nervous of the unfamiliar weight.

"Shh, Ruby!" Beatrice went to Ruby's nose and calmed him. "It's all right."

Petroc bit his lip and gathered up the reins. Ruby was tense, ready to bolt, and that would be a disaster.

"Push up with your left leg so you can settle in the saddle and face forward." That was easier said than done. "Wriggle!" she commanded. "Only your right leg is turned inwards. Your body should face the horse's ears."

He wriggled, mortified. This cursed saddle was a torture device.

But she was right. As he wriggled around so that his hip bones faced forwards, suddenly everything stopped hurting. Except his leg. Pushed up against the saddle, caught between the two pommels…it ached damnably.

But he was *on* a horse! A surge of triumph went through him; he could feel the smile on his face. Rubicon settled with Beatrice at his head, but Petroc could still feel the tension in his hindquarters. He patted Ruby's neck, but that didn't help. A ripple went through the chestnut's back as though he were preparing to buck. What had Bob said about no one but Beatrice being able to ride him? What was a woman doing, riding a stallion, anyway? Though she had handled him like an expert…

"I'll lead you for a little way." Her voice was hesitant. Of course she expected him to refuse that – what man wanted to be on a leading rein? But better that than being thrown. That might split his healing wounds right open.

Petroc handed over the reins. "Good idea." He firmed his mouth and pushed his hips down into the saddle. After all, a cavalry officer rode without hands, often – he'd trained in guiding the horse mainly with his seat and knees. Presumably a lady's horse had also been trained to respond to the pressure of a single knee.

Beatrice walked them down the hill, his crutches in one hand, Rubicon picking his way with more energy than he needed. The horse was clearly torn between bucking him off and pleasing Beatrice—pleasing her won by a hair. And why not? Who wouldn't want to please her?

For a moment, the idea of pleasing— of *pleasuring*—Beatrice took his breath away.

What a cad he was! Such imaginings were more suited to a green boy than a man his age. She turned and smiled up at him encouragingly, and he smiled back with an effort. She was out of his stars. Look at him – on a woman's horse, being lead while the woman carried his crutches. He'd never felt less like a man in his life.

Still…Ruby's muscles bunched and relaxed under him. His leg hurt like the devil, but it was worth it to have this sense of *ease* in moving over the landscape.

He drew in a big breath of sea air and let it out again. Was he prepared to make a fool of himself, to be the butt of wits and goosecaps, in order to ride? Would he? In order to feel free again?

Would he!

Beatrice stopped just before they reached the road, in the shelter of a small copse of hazel. Carefully, he eased his right knee out of its cradle. It was swollen, and it hurt to the touch. Ah well. One paid for one's pleasures.

Kicking free of the stirrup, he jumped down. He tried to do it gracefully – or at least *competently*—but he stumbled. Beatrice was there, holding him steady. Her body against his. Just for a moment. He swallowed and took a breath, which she misinterpreted.

"Oh, Captain, I'm sorry! You're hurt!"

"No, no, not at all." Free of its restraint, his leg was flaring into real pain, but he'd felt worse than this. He took the crutches from her, immediately feeling more stable.

"This was a mistake." She regarded him anxiously.

"I think it may not be the answer. But perhaps I need to heal more before I try it again."

"Well. Proof you can do it, at least. That

you'll be able to ride again." Her smile was worth all the pain.

Swinging his crutches carefully as they made their way back to the road, he looked out over the sweep of the inlet with more hope than he'd felt since Waterloo. If he could only *ride* …free again!

CHAPTER 6

Sitting in a garden like a landlubber, Petroc grinned to himself, still cock-a-hoop.

"You look pleased with yourself."

His youngest brother let himself in the gate and came over, grinning back at him. Ives. Twenty now, and filled out, as the Trengrouse men did around his age. Good shoulders on him, but his dark hair was a bit long. Perhaps that was the fashion for non-military men now.

And for some reason, he seemed to be very damp.

"Brother," Petroc said. "A little wet out?"

"Bloody Den Kelynack. Stranded me out on Grey Rock and I had to swim back, my boots stuffed down my shirt. My good boots! They'll never be the same." He brooded a little as Petroc laughed. Den had been *his* friend before he'd enlisted. It was good to know his talent for mischief was as strong as ever.

"I'll get him back, though," Ives said, eyes mirthful. "I have a *plan.*"

Petroc laughed again, and wondered at himself. Ives grinned.

"We were bringing the *Sally-Ann* over from our cove. At least Den left her tied up with the Smiths in Swain Cove," Ives said, leaning up against the bower upright. "I thought you might like to take her out now she's yours again."

The *Sally-Ann* had been his boat. A two-hander, although one could sail her alone in a pinch. He'd left her with Ives when he went into the Army.

"She was a present, not a loan," he said. Ives smiled at him, a slow smile.

"That's very nice of you, brother, but no need. I'm flush and I'm thinking of buying myself a yacht."

"She's not much use to me now," Petroc said, indicating his stump.

"She's a sailing boat! You don't *walk* her around, you sail her! Look at old Josiah Smith—he lost his leg at Trafalgar, and he's still the best sailor in the cove!"

Best sailor and best smuggler. Ives was right; still, Josiah had a peg-leg, and he'd need one of those, to brace himself as they tacked. He said so to Ives.

"Right! So when you get your wooden foot, we'll take her out together."

Petroc nodded. "She'll be *our* boat."

Ives clapped him on the shoulder. "I'm off. If I stay any longer the old lady will invite me to tea, and I'm in no fit case to be anyone's visitor. I'd hate to drip salt water on her rug!"

They shook hands and Ives took himself off, whistling.

What a day. A day when the world opened up to him, on land and on sea.

BEATRICE LEFT the captain sitting under the bower while she took Ruby around to the stables. The poor man was white as a sheet. What a fool she was! He had looked so tired up on the hill, she'd thought nothing of putting him up on Ruby – but the saddle pommels were sized for her leg, not a man's, and must have pinched cruelly.

She'd never forgive herself if she'd put back his recovery.

Bob came out to take Ruby, but she waved him away. "The captain is in the front garden. He's…we put him up on Ruby, and now his leg…go and see if he needs assistance."

Bob nodded. "I won't let him stop me, miss." He headed off at a run.

Dear Bob. He'd always been quick of understanding. He'd take the captain in hand and make that stubborn man look after himself. Relieved, she led Ruby into his stall, unsaddled him and rubbed him down, waiting until he was cool to give him water. Not that he had to cool down much – that slow, steady walk had done most of it.

Should she go to see how the captain was? Would he think she was fussing? Her father and brother had *hated* fussing. That was probably why her parents had been so perfect for each other; a less fussy woman than Mama was hard to imagine.

She should change first. If Mama saw her with horse hair all over her riding habit… besides, it was time for her to put the house in order before dinner.

Changing quickly in her room, she brushed down her habit and put it carefully away, then dressed in an old round gown so she could tidy and dust the main rooms. She'd grown accustomed to it now. Mrs Marrak couldn't do it all on her own, even though she got a girl in from the village for the weekly scrub and polish.

Beatrice did many of the duties of a parlour maid or butler: tidying, dusting, laying the fires. She had even learnt how to polish silver herself!

She hated it. She was ashamed of hating it. After all, servants had been doing these things for her all her life. What right did she have to hate it so?

It wasn't the work so much as the sheer *boredom* of it. Every day the same. No one but Mama to talk to, and what was there to talk about? Nothing happened in Swain Cove.

Well, nothing happened that anyone would tell *her* about. Not even Charity, who kept so many secrets as the vicar's daughter it was astonishing she didn't burst with them!

If there had been a lending library anywhere near, or if they were able to afford new books...or to keep Ruby... Riding had always been her main delight. Riding, training the young horses, working on the breeding with their estate manager… Today had been like a golden gift from the past.

But Ruby must be sold.

She lit the fire in the drawing room and stood looking at it in a thoroughly despondent mood.

CHAPTER 7

The next day, the captain sent Bob to Trengrouse Hall to pick up his mail and take letters to his parents; from him, and from Beatrice's mother.

There was a postal receiving office here in one of the inns, but the letters went from here to Portsmouth and then out again, and would probably take a fortnight before they got to the Hall.

"I should have written weeks ago," he admitted, flushing. "But I had nothing to say."

She was pleased that now he did; riding again was news indeed, even if it had hurt. In their circle, a man who couldn't ride was… lesser than others. Which was a ridiculous position for a man like the captain to be in.

His own mail wasn't the only thing Bob brought back. There was a letter for her mother from the countess.

"Your mother has invited us all to stay at Trengrouse Hall for a few days," Mama said to the captain as they sat down for afternoon tea. Her face, as always, gave nothing away; the perfect lady. Beatrice had so often wished her own expressions were as beautifully controlled. She *tried*, she really did, but she couldn't match Mama's composure.

The captain stopped dead, emotions flickering over his face almost too fast to catch. Then he bowed at Mama and sat. He was becoming better at doing that; his early clumsiness gradually being smoothed out.

Beatrice sat also. Trengrouse Hall. She'd been there with her mother before, just after her come-out. The captain must have been in Portugal then. It was a huge, rambling old house, full to the brim with family, friends and business acquaintances. Beatrice wasn't sure she wanted to face all of them, in their current poverty-stricken state.

On the other hand – people! Life! Parties and music and conversation that wasn't about gardening! And much better than the Assemblies Charity had been so hesitant to offer her.

"How kind of her," Beatrice said. Besides her on the sofa, the captain was tense. In pain from the ride? It wouldn't be surprising. He'd pushed himself far more than was wise for a first try.

"Me too?" he asked. Mrs Marrak came in with the tea tray and put it down in front of Mama, who began to pour.

"Of course! But not to worry – she writes that she understands you need to continue with the sea bathing here, and will only steal you for the party. Your sister's eighteenth?"

"Oh. Yes. Kerenza." He didn't seem happy at the idea. Perhaps facing the whole family was a little daunting. Beatrice smiled at him encouragingly.

"It's very kind of your mother to include us. You can show me all your favourite spots."

He grinned at her, quickly, as though he couldn't help it. "When are we to go, ma'am? My sister's birthday is on the 26th."

"Yes. So your mother would like us there by the 23rd. It will be quite a large affair, I think. She writes that she will welcome my help." Ten days away.

"No one plans such things as you do, Mama." Her mother gave a one-shouldered shrug. Odd. Bea would have thought that she'd be delighted to visit her old friend.

Beatrice sped through dressing for dinner so she could tap at her mother's door.

"Come!"

Mama was standing in front of the cheval glass, studying her reflection. Her puce satin dress was two years old, like most of Bea's. Her mother had bought it a few months before their family was destroyed, and it was one of only a few which hadn't been dyed black for mourning, because it was feared its elaborate lace wouldn't take the dye evenly.

"You look lovely, Mama. Don't worry about your clothes – I'm sure we can refurbish our old ones. Charity's Mama gets *La Belle Assemblée*. We can see what the latest trends are and fripperise accordingly."

"Beatrice! "Fripperise!" I very much doubt that is a word." Her mother frowned, and turned from the mirror. "In any case, I care very little about what clothes are fashionable. I dressed to please your father, no one else." Mama looked her over and frowned. "You are correct, however. We will need to refurbish our gowns. I have some money put aside for that."

"You *do*?"

"Just a little. I sold my opal ring. I never liked it; opals are unlucky. I thought there might come a time when you wanted to return to Society, and-" She straightened and took a deep breath. "And I was determined I would be ready to chaperone you when the time came. The time has come, it seems."

"Trengrouse Hall isn't exactly Society, Mama. It will be full of our friends."

"Close enough." Her mother's voice was wry. Odd.

She couldn't think about that now. Clothes. They had to have clothes for the visit to Trengrouse Hall, and apparently they had some money for the purpose.

Shopping tomorrow, then. An unexpected treat.

She straightened her back until it was as upright as her mother's, and went down to dinner.

CHAPTER 8

Shopping. How had he come to this? In St Austell, of all places. Scarcely a mercantile hub.

But the ladies had needed to go, and he had no present for Kerenza, so they'd borrowed Mrs Hope's landau, gone the long way around by road, and here they were.

Perhaps Kerenza would like that Indian sapphire he'd brought back from France, set in a ring or pendant.

Something in him shied away from that idea. No, he'd buy her a painted fan or a pair of earrings or somesuch.

The dowager and Beatrice—when had he started to think of her as simply "Beatrice", he wondered—picked their way down the sometimes uneven paving of the main street, towards the haberdashery. It galled him that he couldn't lend them an arm each to steady them – but that would put them all sprawling in the gutter. He grinned internally at the image that presented, but the thought was bitter. And people stared so!

For the first time, getting that wooden leg felt like something to be wished for. He'd surely be less conspicuous with a simple limp than he was stumping along on his crutches.

He left the ladies at the door of the haberdasher's, and made it across the muddy street to a jeweller's. God only knew what he'd find there, but he might be in luck.

Otherwise…hmm…Kerenza, at eighteen, was entirely dependent on his father. The girls weren't given shares in the mines as the boys had been on their fifteenth birthdays. He stopped outside the jeweller's door. He'd become all too aware over the past few weeks of what it was like, being dependent on others.

And Beatrice…if her brother had thought ahead and made provision for her, she'd be in much better case now.

He would sign over a parcel of his shares to Kerenza. He could manage them for her, if she chose. But Keri was a canny lass. She might enjoy taking an interest in the business. And he could afford it. His salary from the Peninsula campaign had gone virtually untouched, so he had invested it in a new steam engine company, and had already doubled his money.

The post office was nearby. He bought paper and stamps and wrote a note to his man of business in London to expedite the change of ownership and to send the shares down to him at Trengrouse Hall.

He looked forward to seeing Kerenza's face when he gave them to her—perhaps this visit to the Hall wouldn't be as bad as he feared.

In the carriage, on the way home, Beatrice asked him what he had bought his sister, and he explained his decision.

"An excellent idea!" She nodded with real approval; his heart seemed to warm in his chest. The dowager, surprisingly, also nodded.

"Yes. It's a good thing for a girl to have something of her own to fall back on. However, I would advise that you put the shares in a trust for the girl. Out of her husband's control. One never knows when one may need to access funds for oneself."

The two women exchanged a *look*. He was touched with pity, but also admiration. They had dealt with their setbacks with such dignity and poise. True ladies.

And the dowager was right. Kerenza's dowry would become her husband's the minute they married – in fact, everything she owned would become his. But shares put into a trust…that would be safe. If her husband were profligate, or a miser, or a gambler…he was shaken at the thought of how vulnerable a young bride became. It was good he could do something to protect Kerry.

"That's an excellent idea, ma'am. Perhaps you might agree to be one of her trustees? You and my mother, I think, would be appropriate."

The dowager bestowed one of her rare warm smiles on him.

"Very appropriate."

OVER THE NEXT FEW DAYS, he saw Beatrice only at meals. Otherwise, she was entirely involved in preparation for their sojourn at the Hall. Mrs Penhaligon had been there every day, as well.

He had no idea what could take so long… but, of course, they didn't have maids to attend to all of that. How could he not have realised their poverty when their household staff was so small? Not having a maid would seem to his sisters as though the world had ended!

Too caught up in his own misery, that's how. Ashamed, he began to make an effort to help Bob and Mr Marrak. He couldn't cut wood, but he could curry horses and clean tack. The men accepted his help with an air of condescension he found funny.

"Too much time just with the ladies?" Bob diagnosed, grinning at him, the first time he ventured down to the stable

"Something like that." The grin grew wider and Bob handed over a bridle and saddle soap.

Sitting in the stable, working the soap into the old, rich leather, surrounded by the smell of horses and hay, he felt…contented. A different emotion to the wild joy he'd felt on his first ride, but perhaps more promising for the future.

Deep within, he knew that it was Beatrice who had caused the change, and not just be-cause of her encouragement to ride. It was more the way she seemed oblivious to him being crippled – even while she talked about it quite openly. It was an odd combination, but it was curiously freeing.

He moved on to polishing the brass rings on the buckles, and thought it through. Perhaps it was that she treated his lack of leg as simply a practical problem, not a…not a shameful thing.

A practical problem. If he could make *himself* think of it like that, he knew his life would be better.

But he was still very far from that.

MAKING old dresses into new ones wasn't easy for women who'd never sewed anything more complex than an embroidered hand-kerchief or a cross-stitched chair back. Beat-rice's bed was covered with all the dresses they had not dyed black. It was a daunting tumble of silk and satin and muslin, and Beatrice had no idea where to start.

Charity came, with *La Belle Assemblée* under her arm. More usefully, she had done practical sewing all her life.

"For the poor," she explained to Mama. "They're always needing baby clothes."

"I daresay," Mama said faintly. She had turned Beatrice's dressing table stool around so she could supervise their efforts. Poor thing. She was determined to present well at Trengrouse Hall, but, as in all things, her understanding of how to choose clothes was at the highest level – in the past she would have simply gone to the modiste, discussed what she wanted, and walked out.

But, once she had looked at Charity's magazines, she had definite ideas.

"The bustline must come up," she said. "Cut off that train, and the hem goes above the shoes – really, it's quite scandalous, but I suppose one must follow fashion."

"My Mama wouldn't let me show my ankles off," Charity said, as they stared with fascination at the picture of a ballgown where one could almost see the lady's calf.

"The images are an exaggeration, naturally," Mama said. "We will not make it quite so short. Just so that one can see the toes of the dancing slipper."

"It will be a relief not to have to drag a train around while dancing," Beatrice put in.

They got to work on the most important dress first – her own dress for the birthday ball. A blue satin with puffed sleeves, it had a demi-train of lace which Mama carefully removed – all that embroidery had made her skilled at unpicking, at least!

Some new silver riband under the bust to pull it in tighter, matching riband around the sleeves. The train was repurposed into flounces of lace around the hem.

"Beautiful!" Charity said when Beatrice tried it on. Beatrice looked at herself in the cheval glass. She knew she wasn't fashionably pretty – she'd have to be slight and blonde for that. But she looked well. What would Captain Trengrouse think of her? He might be beyond her reach, but she would like to see that look of admiration in his eyes, as it had been when she'd encountered him on the clifftop.

"Good," her mother said. "Take that one off and we'll get started on a walking costume for you."

"But Mama, your gown should be next!"

"My dear, I'm a dowager. I'll be sitting in the corner with all the other chaperones. No one will care what I wear."

"Nonsense!" But her mother held firm. They could refurbish her gowns with whatever time and ribands they had left. It was Beatrice who must look her best.

Belatedly, Beatrice realised that her mother saw this trip as an opportunity for her to make a match. Her stomach dipped at the thought, and yet…if it took marriage to get out of here… The ideal would be to marry someone who had a London townhouse as well as an estate, so that she and Mama could go back to the life she had known, away from the stifling boredom of Swain Cove.

Yes. That was the best outcome. And if she had to marry a Cit…well, she could always talk him into buying such an estate.

But that night, in her dreams, she was dancing with Petroc Trengrouse – an odd, hoppity kind of dance because he had a wooden leg, but they were both laughing and happy and her heart filled to bursting with something she couldn't name.

She lay in the early sunlight the next morning and heard the gate and that odd step-thump of his walk, as he left for the cove.

Then she buried her face in the pillow and cried.

CHAPTER 9

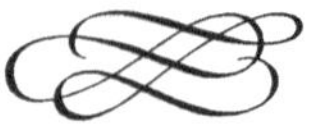

Trengrouse Hall. Granite for strength, but only three stories, to avoid the worst of the winter storms. Sprawling, in so many styles it essentially had none, it had been home to generations of Trengrouse, going back to before the creation of the first earl after the Civil War.

Petroc had come back to it many times over the years, and always before it had felt welcoming. But sitting in the barouche beside the ladies instead of cantering on the green sward beside the gravel drive...his heart clenched at meeting all his old friends, and watching them try to either ignore or make a joke out of his injury. At least none of his male friends would show any sympathy. That just wasn't done.

As they approached, his father came out to greet them.

The Earl of Trengrouse was in his sixties now, upright and with a full head of strong grey hair, his eyes as bright as ever. Bob was there to help Petroc down, and stand ready with his crutches, but then his father stepped forward and embraced him, a thing which hadn't happened in his memory. He fought back tears.

"Papa," he managed.

His father swallowed hard, and nodded, moving back. "You look…better."

How bad had he looked before, to get this response? Pretty bad, evidently.

"I'm feeling much better."

"Good, good." Papa turned to greet the ladies, with great warmth.

"Abigail," he said, bowing for only a moment and then taking the dowager's arm to escort her into the house. "And little Beatrice!"

"Not so little any more, Uncle Jory."

He chuckled as they walked four abreast to the wide entrance steps his grandfather had put in. "No, no. We must find you a husband while you're here! Keep you in Cornwall."

"That's an excellent idea," the dowager said. "I knew I could rely on you, Jory."

He had no right to feel cold as ice at that idea, Petroc told himself. No right at all. Beatrice might accept his handicap in a practical way, but that didn't mean she would want a cripple for a husband. He wasn't fit to marry anyone.

Pull yourself out of that frame of mind! He couldn't be in a foul mood when he met Mama.

He had to go to the side of the steps and use the handrail, but he pushed himself so he reached the top at the same time as the others. Beatrice cast him an admonitory glance, but she smiled as she shook her head at him.

Mr Carveth, their butler, had the double doors standing open ready for them. He was the opposite of the London butlers Petroc had encountered: short and wiry where they were tall and stately, and full of beans where they were impassive. He winked at Petroc as they came through the doors, and Petroc winked back. Carveth had hidden any number of childhood scrapes from their parents; he was a good man to have on one's side.

Then Mother was there, and Kerenza, and Ives and Locryn and…everyone. It was overwhelming, as they swarmed over him, hugging and patting his shoulder and shaking his hand.

The dowager looked a little overwhelmed, too.

"Back off, you lot!" he ordered his siblings. "Try to act like you have some manners."

"Ooh, the Army captain is giving us orders!" Kerenza giggled.

"Yes, sir!" Endellion saluted him while his brothers laughed and Melissa smiled.

But they backed off and followed their parents and guests into the great chamber, a huge place which fulfilled the functions of drawing room, morning room and ballroom, once the furniture was removed. There were more intimate drawing rooms, but for the full family to fit, the great chamber was necessary.

Beatrice knew his sisters, of course. She and Melissa had come out together and made their curtseys to the queen at the same Drawing-Room. Demelza was the older sister, only living here because her husband had recently died. It had been her idea for him to stay with the Marlowes to recover.

Melza was more straightforward than Beatrice, and he wondered how Beatrice would take his sister's forthright manners, but they were soon chatting away over tea, and Melissa and Keri joined them.

It was strangely warming, having the

whole family together. Felix was the only brother missing.

"He's over at the mine," his father explained as he passed Petroc a glass of ale. (His father was convinced that tea maudled a man's insides.) "We've been having some trouble with getting air in. He's trying to see if we can use the water pumps to push air in as they take water out."

"Sounds complicated."

"Oh, Felix'll manage it. Born for the job."

Father had once said that about him – born to be a soldier. So what could he do now? Petroc pushed that thought away, but it was as though his father heard it, because he hitched his chair nearer, and lowered his voice.

"We need to have a chat, lad. I have an idea or two you might be interested in. When you have a moment."

He nodded, but winced inwardly. The whole family, since Waterloo, had treated him with kid gloves. In the past, his father would simply have ordered him to show up at a particular time.

"Petroc? You know the Misters Muffet, don't you?" his mother asked.

Muffet? He had a vague recollection of the man being in business with his father. Something about tinware?

The two men were clearly father and son. The same fine, mussed brown hair. The same pale blue eyes. The same unfortunate pug nose. The older man was dressed like a Cit: good solid black breeches with an old-fashioned frock-coat. The younger was in the height of fashion, including a high collar and skin-tight yellow breeches over a damnably fine pair of calves. Petroc was pierced by a sudden shaft of envy. He'd never be able to wear pantaloons like that again. It was Petersham's ridiculous long trousers for him from now on.

He conceived an immediate dislike for the younger Mr Muffet. And that had nothing to do with how charmingly Beatrice smiled at him as they were introduced.

But the poor bastard, with a name like that.

IT WAS AS THOUGH she'd gone back in time. As soon as they walked into Trengrouse Hall, she had once again become Lady Beatrice, debutante. The fact that her debut was now more than two years ago was irrelevant. She wasn't betrothed or married; all the strict rules applying to green girls applied to her.

Smile, curtsey, engage in idle chit-chat, smile again. Demurely.

She felt as though she were choking. Even seeing Melissa again gave little relief, being under the eagle eyes of both their mamas.

And Petroc's family were engaged on a concerted campaign to find out how he was, without asking him directly. Their enquiries were aimed at her.

"How are you coping with my ill-tempered big brother?" Kerenza asked, shooting a mischievous look at the captain.

"He's not ill-tempered with me." Beatrice kept her gaze away from his clever brown eyes. "He's always a perfect gentleman."

"Oho!" exclaimed a younger lad. Ives, that would be. Melissa's twin. "You must be a miracle-worker, my lady."

The Muffets looked a little left out, so she exerted herself to ask them about their connections with the Trengrouses. Unsurprisingly, they were in business.

"We make tinware from the Trengrouse tin," the younger Mr Muffet explained. "We're here to discuss a new enamelling process."

"And to come to my party!" Kerenza said, smiling kindly at him. He blushed, sweetly. Odd to think he would be a year or so older than Beatrice herself. She felt much older.

Mr Muffet was deep in conversation with the countess, occasionally looking their way. Hard to see if he was checking on his son, or looking at her and the Trengrouse girls.

"Lots of people will be staying," Demelza

said. She, too, was being kind to him. There was no snobbery from this family; all guests were treated as equally valued.

Mr Muffet-the-younger was relaxing, although his very high shirt-points were wilting slightly. This was obviously not his first meeting with the younger Trengrouses, although they were still formal together. But he was perfectly unexceptional, if a little shy, and Kerenza soon had him laughing about the journey from the Midlands, which according to her was as dangerous as travelling through bandit-infested Sicily.

"I swear, Lady Kerenza, that we're quite civilized in Birmingham! We even have plans for gas lighting in the streets!"

"When you have gas lighting in the *home*, then I might be impressed!"

Which sent the conversation into a debate about whether such a thing could ever happen.

Beatrice was aware of the captain's gaze on them, but he made no effort to join in. He was talking to his father; home again after such an absence, they must have much to discuss. No reason to be disappointed.

She returned her attention to Mr Muffet, who was valiantly defending modern science against any slur the Trengrouse girls could throw at it.

ALMOST TIME TO dress for dinner—Trengrouse Hall kept country hours. Petroc left the gathering first, having no appetite for spectators as he navigated the great staircase.

He passed behind his mother and Mr Muffet senior, who had their heads together. Looking at Beatrice.

"The Earl of Mannering's daughter, yes," his mother said. "A very old line. Only a small dowry, alas, but excellent breeding. Indeed, one could scarcely do better." Surprisingly, she flicked a glance at Petroc. Did she *want* him to hear this?

Mr Muffet nodded his head judicially.

"She seems a very nice young lady. You know her well?"

"I've known her all my life," his mother agreed, "and I have the highest regard for her."

Matchmaking, by God! Petroc swung himself out of the room, unreasonably angry at both of them.

He flung himself at the stairs in a rush of annoyance. Be damned with the handrail. He'd take the stairs with his crutches. How dare they? How dare they spruik Beatrice's good points as though she were a horse for sale?

His crutch slipped on the last step before the landing and he went sprawling, arms out like a scarecrow. The footman in the hall began to race up the stairs, taking them two at a time.

Blast him.

Petroc sat up and waved him off. "It's all right, Bryok. No harm done."

"Yessir." But Bryok hovered until Petroc had dragged himself up off the floor; then he had the impertinence to sweep the crutches up and offer them.

"I'm *fine.*"

"Yes, m'lord." Disbelief clear in his voice. Damn the man. And he *couldn't* damn him—he'd known Bryok since they'd been lads together.

"Honestly, Bry. Nothing hurt but my dignity."

Bryok flashed him a quick, rueful smile and stepped back. "Very good, m'lord."

For the second flight, Petroc hung onto the handrail.

He collapsed on his bed still angry, but mostly at himself. A buffoon, that's what he was. Even the servants laughed at him.

But he knew that was unfair to Bryok, who'd only wanted to help. That was the problem. Not only did everyone want to help, he *needed* the help.

And downstairs, his mother was scheming to marry Beatrice off to a Cit. His anger with her, still simmering, was unreasonable. This kind of matchmaking was normal. The *ton* depended on it. It was Beatrice's best bet for a life out of penury.

Sitting there, he admitted why he was angry.

It was because no one thought *he* would make a good husband for Beatrice. The dowager had never so much as hinted at it, in all these weeks. Beatrice herself never flirted with him. Why would she? She probably didn't even think of him as a man.

He wanted to believe it was just his pride which was hurting so much, but he wasn't someone who could lie, not even to himself. It wasn't wounded pride.

It was love.

Hopeless love.

Pain cracked across his heart. Like the surgeon's knife. He could imagine it – a long, bloody wound right through him. A shame he couldn't have that heart amputated, like his foot.

She deserved better than Muffet. Better than him.

His anger was a too-thin cover over the pain, but he'd take it.

A knock on the door, and Bob popped his head in.

"Ready to dress, capt'n?"

"Yes. Yes, I suppose so." He heaved himself off the bed and pulled off his neckcloth. "Duty calls."

He knew how to do his duty, even when it was so irritating.

"Right you are, sir." Bob helped him take off his scarlet jacket and white waistcoat, but left him tactfully alone for the uniform overalls. A good man, Bob, and a calming presence as he dressed, leaving his uniform behind for formal evening clothes.

"Your old mistress, Bob—Lady Beatrice..."

"Yes, sir?"

"Did she have any beaus before her father died?"

"Oh, yes, sir. House was always full of 'em. But they all shied off once they realised she had no dowry."

"Fools," Petroc muttered. Society was sick if men were turned away from a girl like Beatrice simply because of money. What nodcocks they were! Folderising simpletons, only good for fathering other men's children.

With that bracing thought, he finished his neckcloth, and went carefully down to dinner.

CHAPTER 10

Her mother had requested that they go to dinner together, so Beatrice tapped on her door as soon as she herself was dressed (by a *maid!* What luxury and how shocking that she had always taken it for granted!).

She found her mother staring out the window. Fully dressed, and as beautifully composed as ever. But her eyes were a little red. Had she been crying?

It must be hard, to come back to somewhere she had often visited with Papa.

Beatrice took her hand and squeezed it gently. "Are you all right, Mama?"

There was an expression on her mother's face Beatrice had never seen before. Mama waved a vague hand.

"It's just that I dread parties so."

"What? I mean, I beg your pardon?" This made no sense. Had her mother run mad? Their home had been full of party after party – and if not in their house, her parents had visited their friends' parties. Balls, routs, al fresco entertainments… "Mama, you spent your *life* at parties!"

"*Exactly*! And just when I thought I was free of them at last, this visit! And I couldn't say no, because she's my oldest friend!"

Beatrice plumped down on the bed, astonished. "But, Mama, you *never* said. Never complained."

Mama sat down at the desk, moving the chair so she could face Beatrice. Her normally pale face was flushed; was that embarrassment?

"While I was with your father, I could

bear it. He understood, and would always find a place at every entertainment I could be alone with him and catch my breath now and then. That was why we never put card tables in the library at home. But now he's *gone* and I just can't do it!"

It was almost a wail.

Beatrice"s world turned upside down and shook itself into a new shape, one full of mingled compassion and admiration. No one would *ever* have guessed that the elegant Countess of Mannering hated Society. Admittedly, her public persona was more regal and aloof than her gentle family demeanour. But that was just – *noblesse oblige.*

Helplessly, Bea embraced her mother and patted her on the back. She couldn't think of a single thing to say which didn't sound ridiculous.

"And it has been so *lovely* at Swain Cove!" Mama hiccupped.

In a flash, the last months rearranged themselves in Beatrice's mind. Her mother's continued insistence that she was "perfectly fine" sitting and reading in their parlour or embroidering in the garden. Beatrice had assumed that was Mama being a lady, concealing any pain or dissatisfaction to avoid distressing her household.

It had been *real*, that satisfaction. For someone who hated parties, the quiet monotony of life in Swain Cove might be bliss.

"You don't have to go downstairs. We could send some polite excuse."

Mama straightened up and wiped her cheeks resolutely. "Nonsense. Maria is my oldest friend. I'm sure I can manage a few days. It's a big house. There must be places to retreat to." She smiled reassuringly up at Beatrice. "I suppose our interlude at Swain Cove was too perfect to last." She trailed out the door while Beatrice stood, glued to the spot. *Perfect*? How could she have misunderstood her own mother so badly?

She felt sick. Her stomach roiled in some mixture of pain and foreboding. If her mother loved their life, where did that leave her? She had vaguely thought about marrying and shaking the dust of this village off her feet; but of course she'd imagined taking her mother out of there too.

If her mother wanted to *stay*…Beatrice couldn't seem to get her breath. The room closed in on her, and she swayed on her feet. Buried alive without any hope of escape. She couldn't leave her mother alone. Impossible. Thrusting aside the panic, she put on her public face and followed her mother down the stairs.

All through dinner, her mother held to a perfect demeanour and unruffled calm. Being a lady. Was that all a lie? Beatrice had tried so hard to live up to Mama's example. To be as calm and controlled as a lady should be, despite her own instinct for more vivacity.

But, in the light of this new understanding, she had to ask: was that how a lady should act, after all? Was her mother's behaviour an example to live up to? Or merely a desperate attempt to crush an emotion which might cause embarrassment or distress to others?

The Trengrouse women were all ladies, but none of them, not even the countess, were as composed as Mama. Beatrice wished, suddenly and fiercely, for a sister. If she'd had a sister or even a brother to laugh and tease, as Petroc was teasing Melissa, would she too have found a more relaxed way to present herself?

Food for thought.

CHAPTER 11

"Once more into the breach," Petroc muttered, taking the reins from Bob.

"For Harry, England, and St George!" Beatrice finished the speech he had quoted and smiled up at him with perfect confidence. His whole body warmed at her gaze. Was her smile warmer? Not the time to think about that, with this challenge before him.

Goldie stood placidly at the mounting block, waiting. And on her, not a side saddle but the old hunting saddle his grandfather had used, with its high pommel and dish-shaped seat. That had been Beatrice's idea. She nodded at him encouragingly.

"You'll be right, sir." Bob grinned. "The old earl used to ride home drunk as a sailor in one of those. You can't fall out if you try!"

It had to be better than sidesaddle. The pressure bruises from his one ride on Ruby had taken days and days to heal. He might have some trouble guiding his mount, but Goldie was his old, much-loved, first "big horse", from when he was fourteen and hit his growth spurt. She'd be patient with a rider learning new skills.

Before he could move forward, there was a clatter of boots on the floor, and the younger Mr Muffet came in with Kerenza.

Blast it. He wasn't going to make a cake of himself in front of that puppy. His hands clenched on the crutches.

He turned away from Goldie only to see Beatrice move forward.

"Mr Muffet! Have you come to ride?"

The man looked surprised; what a slow-top. It was an obvious question.

"No, no," he stuttered. "Lady Kerenza was showing me, um-"

"I wanted to show him Blackfoot's new colt," Kerenza cut in.

"Oh, I'd like to see that too!" Beatrice said. She gave Petroc an unreadable look and shepherded Muffet and Kerenza out the door into the stableyard.

Well. *Well*. He pushed down an odd ache in his chest. If she preferred Muffet to him—well, who wouldn't prefer watching a new foal to seeing him clumsily hoist himself aboard an old nag? And Muffet…he was his father's offsider, apparently. Plump in the pocket thanks to the manufactories his father owned. A good prospect for a girl like her.

She was being sensible. Looking after her future, and her mother's future.

Doing what ladies do: make an advantageous marriage. A shaft of anger and something else—pain?—pierced him down to his fingertips. Bedamned to that. Bedamned to love. He was here to ride.

He set his mouth and hoisted himself onto the mounting block, handed one crutch to Bob and used the other to steady himself while he put his left foot in the stirrup. And then he was on, the familiar motion of mounting taking over without a thought from him. At least that was going right.

Bob was at the bridle, eyes sharp.

Petroc clicked his tongue and Goldie walked forward, ears pricked, and they moved out of the stable block into the sunlight.

His leg could feel the pressure of the knee roll, but it wasn't too bad. A bit bumpy, but he could grip with his knee, at least. It was an odd sensation. Unsettling, to feel his knee, and the salt wind cutting through his thin trousers to chill his stump.

"Let her go, Bob." Bob stepped back, a wary eye on him. "Come on, Goldie." She moved off slowly across the flagstones, heading for the gate onto his favourite ride towards the sea. It brought back so many memories. Bob let them through the gate.

He tensed his leg muscles to prevent his calf from thwacking Goldie, and the horse took that as a signal to speed up.

Petroc leaned forward instinctively, to ease the horse's spine, and found it much easier to keep his seat.

A trot was impossible without two feet in the stirrup, but a gentle canter... As he moved over the brow of the hill and the sea came into view, he pressed his knees into Goldie's sides. He bumped a couple of times as she increased her speed, but then the smooth gait he remembered made it easy.

He whooped like a boy, blood fizzing with excitement.

He thrust a thought of riding here with Beatrice out of his mind. She was better off with Muffet than she could ever be with him.

And at least he could ride again.

.   .   .

BEATRICE SHEPHERDED Mr Muffet and Kerenza away from the captain. He shouldn't have spectators for his first proper ride. So mortifying. Particularly a stranger like Mr Muffet.

Who was chatting with surprising familiarity with Kerenza.

He seemed like a nice young man, but she hoped he wasn't indulging in hopes in that direction. The Earl was unlikely to approve his daughter marrying beneath her. The Mr Muffets of the world were fine for *her,* though—oh yes, she'd seen the countess put her head together with the senior Muffet.

Selling her off.

Her emotions were so contradictory she couldn't sort them out. Anger, hope, despair, more anger. And underneath, a yearning to be with Petroc, to make sure he was all right. How *stupid* of her, to fall in love like this with a man she couldn't have!

"Look!" Kerenza cried. "Isn't he adorable?"

For a stunned moment, Beatrice thought

she meant Mr Muffet, and almost laughed. But it was the foal, of course, a few months old now and racing across the paddock with his tail held high.

The three of them leant on the fence and watched.

"Nice conformation," Beatrice said. "What's his breeding?"

"By Hartigan out of Blackfoot." The dam, a bay who did have remarkably black feet, was grazing placidly. "Blackfoot traces back to the Godolphin Barb, and Hartigan's from the Smetanka line."

"How on Earth did your father achieve that?" Beatrice was impressed. Smetanka was an Arab stallion from Russia, and the bloodline was jealously guarded.

"Oh, you know Father. Favours here, favours there, and things happen. He bought a mare in foal from them, and luckily it was a colt."

Mr Muffet was looking confused, poor thing.

"We're boring Mr Muffet," she said. "Not everyone is horse-mad."

"They are in this family." Kerenza wrinkled her nose. "I like them when they're tiny, but I do get tired of all the breeding rigmarole."

"You like to ride, though, Lady Kerenza," Mr Muffet said tentatively.

"Well, of course!"

Kerenza seemed astonished at the question. She walked off to get a better look at the colt at the head of the pasture. Mr Muffet watched her leave with an expression that was hard to read.

"Have you known the Trengrouses long, Mr Muffet?"

He turned to her with a charming smile. "Most of my life, Lady Beatrice. Our fathers have been in business together for quite some time, and I used to come with him when he visited. Until I went to school."

So, he was relying on boyhood relationships and finding that they didn't get him far now. Poor man.

"Now you have the fun of getting to know them all as adults," she suggested.

"Indeed." His mouth quirked in a wry smile. "Enough about the Trengrouses! Tell me about yourself, Lady Beatrice. You live near here, I believe?"

They slid into ordinary conversation. He was a sensible man, intelligent and well-read. Beatrice would have enjoyed herself if her mind hadn't constantly gone to Petroc. Wondering if he'd managed the ride. If he'd hurt his leg. If he would be downcast or ebullient when they next met.

Mr Muffet asked her a question.

"I'm sorry. My mind was wandering…"

Kerenza tripped back to them, a smile on her face. "Come on, you two! Stop cozing! It's time to decorate the ballroom."

They walked back to the house abreast, with Mr Muffet in the middle. A nice man. If she had any sense at all, she'd set her cap for him.

Convince him to buy an estate where Mama could live quietly in the dower house;

a sanctuary for her which was also close for visits and help if needed.

Yes, that was what she ought to do. Definitely.

Before they went in through the library doors, she craned her neck, but could see no sign of the captain on the trail to the sea.

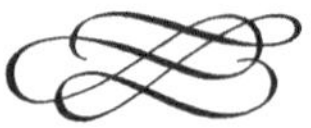

CHAPTER 12

Walking back to the house hurt. Damnably. Every jolt of the crutches sent pain shafting through him.

Petroc didn't care. His heart was still soaring, cantering along the trail back from the sea.

Free again. Once he had his new foot—a matter of weeks—he'd be free. Free to walk, rather than stump along. Free to ride. Free to move easily and quickly and go anywhere he chose.

It would help if he had any idea what he wanted to do. All he was sure of was that he didn't want the office job his father had offered.

The post had arrived, including a letter from his man of business in London, which Mr Carveth handed to him when he came into the hall. Kerenza's shares. Excellent.

"Miss Kerenza is in the ballroom," Mr Carveth said.

He nodded, opening the letter and extracting the relevant share documents. "I wouldn't mind a drink, Mr Carveth. Have Bryok bring it there?"

"Certain sure, Mr Petroc."

Mister. He'd have to get used to that, too. Technically his title had been Captain the Honourable Petroc Trengrouse, but no one in Hookey's army used honorifics or titles. He'd been simply "Captain" and proud of it. Going back to "Mister" felt like a demotion.

In the ballroom, Elestryn, Locryn's wife, all his sisters, and Beatrice were assembling huge flower arrangements which would sit on pedestals in niches along the walls. Mr Muffet, damn him, was helping, and causing some hilarity by his ineptness at flower arranging.

Beatrice looked up and saw him. Time seemed to slow down, as it did sometimes in battle. She saw him. Her eyes grew intent as she assessed his condition. Then she smiled.

His heart thumped and stopped for a long moment. Thumped again, so hard it almost hurt. He smiled back. Her grey eyes warmed and that warmth spread through his whole body.

Melissa thrust a basket of phlox into his hands, the strong scent making him sneeze, and it was as though that moment hadn't happened.

All the Trengrouse men were used to being ordered around by their sisters. It was easier to just give in from the start.

His crutches saved him from the worst fetching and carrying, but they put him sitting next to Beatrice at a small table as she constructed astonishing works of art.

"Where did you learn flower arranging?"

She grinned at him – yes, it was a positive

grin, not just the ladylike smile he was used to.

"My Mama believes that 'every young gel should learn to arrange flowers'. She's very good at it. She doesn't have much scope for it at the Semper House, but at home she had acres of flower gardens to draw on."

Her face clouded for a moment, and she looked involuntarily at Mr Muffet. So she was thinking about him as a marriage prospect. Someone who could provide acres of flower gardens for her and her mother.

He couldn't sit here and watch it. He hoisted himself up and found Kerenza.

"Happy Birthday, Keri." She put her hand out and looked surprised to be given papers instead of a present.

"But-these are shares." Astonished, all the girls crowded around.

"Yes," he said. "Held in trust for you. Mama and Lady Marlowe are your trustees. It should provide you with a little independent income."

Kerenza's eyes grew wide.

"Th-thank you."

Five pairs of eyes stared at him.

He was filled with a sense of having done an enlightened and generous thing. It gave him pause. Since Waterloo, it had felt as though he'd never be good for anything, ever again. Riding had helped, but it was…personal. Giving Kerenza shares was the first time he'd reached out to perform an action in the wider world. He'd been curled up somewhere safe, licking his wounds like a dog.

It felt good to do something real.

"Why Kerenza?" Demelza asked. Uh-oh. Think fast, man!

"I thought I'd talk to the others—Locryn and the others—and see if we couldn't find parcels of shares for all of you. It's not good for a woman to be completely dependent on her husband. Or on getting a husband."

Beatrice stood up from her table. Mr Muffet was staring at him as though he was mad.

"It certainly isn't," Elestryn said. "That was well thought of."

"You'll set a trend," Mr Muffet said. "I hope my sisters don't hear about this—it might bankrupt us!"

Petroc chuckled. "Do you have many?"

"Six!" Muffet said in tones of despair.

Everyone laughed.

Damn the man, he didn't have to be pleasant as well as rich. He'd been underestimating the junior Mr Muffet.

Mr Carveth brought in refreshments, and the decorating was declared done.

The room did look good, with afternoon sun streaming through the long doors which led out to the terrace. He wished he didn't have to attend. Watching everyone else dance would be…bad. He'd loved dancing.

No time for maudlin thoughts. Today was the day he'd ridden again. The future wasn't as bleak as he'd thought.

Beatrice came over, a glass of lemonade in her hand. "How did your ride go?"

"Well." He couldn't help it, he grinned at her. "Very well." Then his mood darkened. "I hope Mr Muffet enjoyed seeing Blackfoot's colt?"

"Oh, Petroc, really. I took them away so you wouldn't have any spectators." He was a fool. An addle-pated fool. He should have known she'd never abandon him. "I'm so glad your ride went well."

She smiled; and this time it was a personal, emotion-filled smile. Happiness for him, affection, and understanding.

"That colt has excellent conformation," she added. "Wonderful stock. Smetanka!"

He blinked. He'd known she was a rider, but most women didn't comment on horse *breeding*—perhaps they thought it was indelicate.

"It was a coup of Father's," he acknowledged.

"I'd have loved to bring that bloodline into our breeding programme at Mannering," she said wistfully.

"I'll show you the stud books in the morning, if you'd like."

"Oh, yes! I'd love that!" Where had the formal Lady Beatrice gone? This girl glowed with interest and delight. He wanted to touch her cheek in response. To bend and kiss her.

"Beatrice!" Elestryn called. "These vases are just beautiful!"

Beatrice touched his hand where it gripped the crutch, and moved away.

Soon it would be time for them all to go up to get ready. And then he'd have to sit on the sidelines like a wallflower and watch Beatrice waltz with Muffet.

He turned and clumped out, seeking refuge somewhere—anywhere—that was Muffet-free.

As he left, he turned back for a last glimpse, and there the man was, leaning over Beatrice and Kerenza, laughing. It was a bad angle to look at him from; he looked more like a pug than ever.

Impossible to imagine Beatrice's elegance next to that.

· · ·

How odd, Beatrice thought. When she was with Petroc, it was so easy to slide her trained formality off, like a cloak she no longer needed. But with the others, it came back full force, and she reverted to the kind of composure her mother preferred.

It wasn't just because she cared about him. There was something about *him*. His lack of judgement of others? His acceptance of her as competent and intelligent? Or perhaps it was simply that she knew he'd never marry her, so there was no need to be "delightful".

She didn't know. But, in contrast, Mr Muffet's quiet charm seemed facile.

In full moonlight, carriages trundled to the front steps, disgorged their passengers, and headed for the stables, where another party would no doubt start.

Petroc grinned to himself as he joined the receiving line with his parents. As a boy, too young for balls, he'd sometimes snuck down to the stables and played cards or dice with the coachmen and grooms. It had made him feel so manly, accepted among the horse crowd.

The horse crowd…an idea sparked in his

mind. As he bowed over and over again, he turned it over in his head, hope about the future burgeoning in him for the first time.

At a lull in the visitor line, he bent and spoke to his father. "Papa, could I have a word tomorrow?"

"Certainly. I've been wanting to talk to you." His father fixed him with a shrewd eye. "Heard you went out on Goldie today."

"Yes." Petroc couldn't help the smile that came to his face. "A bit rough and ready, but it will be better once I have the artificial foot."

Papa nodded. "It's all a man needs—a good horse and somewhere to ride."

Perhaps not *all*. Petroc bit back a rather crude comment. His parents did have eight children, after all!

In a flash, he imagined Beatrice as the mother of his children: black haired little ones with clear grey eyes. He shrugged the image away. That could never be. He was an object of pity to her, and perhaps a friend. That was all.

As a friend, he should be encouraging Muffet.

But that he couldn't do.

IT HAD BEEN SO LONG since she'd danced! Beatrice let her feet carry her, her hand in Endellion's. Was he the fourth or the fifth Trengrouse child? Older than her, or younger? She could never keep them all straight in her head.

Older or younger, he was an excellent dancer, and he grinned at her as they crossed in the measure.

After Endelion, it was Ives. And then Mr Muffet, who was less graceful but also less bumptious than Ives.

Which was good, because they were playing a waltz.

Compared to the quadrille which had just ended, waltzing was child's play. She followed Mr Muffet easily; he led well. But he had little to say. His eyes, often, went over her shoulder to something—some*one*—beyond. Kerenza, she'd seen, was dancing with a rather dashing Corinthian.

"You haven't asked Kerenza to dance," she said. He started and lost his footing. They paused for a moment, and then resumed the dance.

"She's promised me the supper dance." His mouth firmed. "And I shall insist that she honours her promise."

Mr Muffet had what her grandmother had called "nothing eyes". Not blue nor grey nor even really hazel. The light in them, though, was clear enough. He was taken with Kerenza. Should she warn him? Yes. He was a kind man, and might not understand the limits of the Trengrouse hospitality.

"The Earl intends to make advantageous marriages for his children," she said.

His gaze sharpened. "You mean Lady Kerenza will never marry a Cit."

"Any more than one of the Trengrouse men will marry a dowerless girl like me."

"A man such as the captain." Humiliated,

she managed to nod. She had embarrassed him in the same way, after all.

The music ended and they paused, hand still in hand.

"Perhaps you're right. My father thinks so, too." He smiled bitterly. "A pact, then, Lady Beatrice. Better to settle for each other than live alone."

She smiled wryly.

"I think you'll have more choices than I will."

He bowed over her hand and released it. "You would be my first choice in that circumstance. Never doubt it."

Beatrice bit back tears and curtseyed. "I think you would be mine, too, Mr Muffet."

As they turned to promenade back to where she and the other young ladies were sitting, she saw Petroc standing nearby, staring daggers. Had he heard?

Mortification brought a blush up from her decolletage. She could feel the heat sweep over her, and raised her chin in defiance of it.

What if he *had* heard? It was no business of his. He'd had *plenty* of opportunity to make advances. So *many* opportunities that it was clear he had no intention of even flirting with her, let alone making an offer.

She had every *right* to seek a husband elsewhere. If she could have stamped her foot, she would have.

However, that wouldn't have been ladylike.

CHAPTER 14

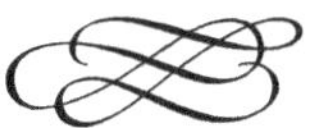

*I*mpossible that Beatrice should marry that mushroom! Petroc thumped the arm of his chair. He wanted to jump up and pace the length of the library where he'd taken refuge, but hopping around would do nothing but make him ridiculous.

The Trengrouses were generally far more tolerant of Cits than most of the ton—they'd been in business themselves for generations, after all. But Muffet…what a name! His aunt had had a dog named Muffet. A fat, mean little thing with a face like Muffet's.

The thought made his face heat with

shame. Muffet wasn't a bad fellow. But he wasn't up to Beatrice's weight, and that was all there was to it.

She *couldn't* be planning to accept him, surely?

"I think you would be mine, too, Mr Muffet," she'd said. Her choice. He'd heard only scraps of their conversation, but he'd heard that.

He leant forwards, his elbows on his knees, and stared at the fire. Her life now was all work and boredom. She'd have to sell Ruby, and then there would be no outlet for that spirit and fire. At least Muffet would take her out of Swain Cove, and she wouldn't have to pinch pennies or pretend she was a parlour maid.

I could give her that.

He could. He was at least as plump in the purse as Muffet, even having given Keri a parcel of his shares.

Surely it would be better, to marry a man of her own kind? Not just class, but thoughts and interests?

Someone who loved her. Hard to admit, but the truth was there, at the centre of his anger and yearning. He loved Lady Beatrice Marlowe more than ever. Not the restrained, quiet, ladylike face she presented to the world, but the girl behind that. The one who rode like an Amazon, and grinned up at him, and talked to horses as though they were people.

His heart slowed down, beating hard and heavy, as it did before battle. Could he? Did he *dare*?

Breathe, man. He breathed.

And realised that no, he didn't dare. But the thought remained. He could save her from the likes of Muffet.

Perhaps it was time to become thoroughly traditional.

HE HAD to wait until morning to put his plan into action. *Late* morning, since no one had got to sleep before three the night before.

"Mama?" His mother looked up from

the menu she was checking. She ticked something and handed it to the under-cook.

"Thank you, Tess. Tell Cook that will be fine."

"Yes'm." Tess curtsied and sailed away. The Trengrouse servants never scurried. It was as though his mother's calm dignity had infected them all – except Mr Carveth the butler, who remained resolutely chirpy.

He sat across the table, laying his crutches on the floor. This morning room was where Mama did all her household duties, and its yellow walls shone happily in the summer sun. It would be a hot day.

"What can I do for you, my dear?"

"You can…" He was sick with uncertainty. Was he making a huge mistake? Would Beatrice be insulted?

Worse, would they lose their current friendship, on which he'd come to rely so heavily?

"Petroc?" His mother's voice was kind, as always. Somehow, it strengthened him.

"I need you to do a reconnaissance mission for me, Mama."

"Indeed?" She laughed at him; he couldn't help but smile back. This was the other side of her calm dignity—warmth and laughter.

"Lady Beatrice is thinking about marrying Muffet, isn't she?"

His mother's face stilled, as if surprised. "She may be," she said carefully.

"She deserves the best possible marriage. All the elegancies of life. But without a dowry, we both know she won't attract anyone in the first rank. She'll have to… lower herself, in order to be financially secure …to be frank, Mama, I need you to find out whether she'd prefer a cripple over a Cit."

She caught her breath at the word "cripple", and he felt a kick of shame at distressing her—but it was no more than the truth, after all.

"I know I'm no catch," he added. "But perhaps she'd rather stay with her own kind?"

"You think her poverty might level the

scales for you? Make her consider you when she would otherwise turn away?" Why was her tone so dry? It was a perfectly reasonable idea.

"Exactly."

She rose and planted a kiss on the top of his head. "You, my son, are a complete ninny."

"You don't think she'll agree?" Of course she wouldn't. What woman would take damaged goods when she could have a whole man? He'd been a fool even to think it. A harsh pain twisted his heart. He could barely breathe.

"I think you should ask her yourself."

"Oh, no." No. He...he *couldn't*. Not without some hint of how she might reply. "I can't."

His mother took his hands between her own, as if he were still a child. "My dear, any woman would be proud to be your wife."

He shook his head. "No. That's not true. Mama, you haven't seen people *looking*. Please...just...sound her out."

She sighed. "Very well."

He kissed her hand. "Thank you. I just need…I just need some idea of her thinking."

"A *complete* ninny. And blind to boot."

His mother sailed out of the room and left him *feeling* like a complete ninny. There was no hope. Of course there was no hope. But he'd regret it all his life if he didn't at least *try*.

"So, I agreed to sound you out, my dear," the countess said, and threw her hands in the air and let them fall into her lap. "And report."

"Report?" Beatrice clutched the chair back until her knuckles were white. *Control yourself. Breathe.* How *dare* he? "So, let me make sure I have this straight. He thinks that because I am poor, I will put aside my natural distaste for a *cripple*, and marry him in order to…to…"

"To enjoy the elegancies of life. Instead of marrying a Cit."

If she'd been at home, Beatrice would

have picked up the remarkably ugly Meissen shepherdess on the table next to her, and hurled at the wall.

"I told him he was a complete ninny, but I fear he misunderstood me," the countess added.

"A complete *addle-pate*!" Beatrice paced the length of the room, and turned. "Where is he? Waiting for your *report?*"

A twinkle in her eye, Lady Trengrouse nodded. "In the morning room."

Beatrice swept out without even excusing herself. She didn't care. His mother deserved it. What had she been *thinking*, to convey such a message?

I will eviscerate *him!* She'd never been so angry in all of her life.

THE MORNING ROOM door slammed closed with a *clunk*. He started and turned. Beatrice. High colour in her cheeks, and eyes blazing.

"How *dare* you?"

Oh God no. He sprang up from the table

and almost overbalanced, grabbing at the chair to hold him upright.

"How *dare* you?" she demanded again.

"I'm sorry-" Nausea rose in his throat. If she was so insulted, he had misread her friendship completely. It had been simple pity. The thought was a canker in his gut. He was so far beneath her, then.

"Sorry? *Sorry?* How could you even *think* I'd sell myself to the highest bidder!"

"What? No! That wasn't-" How could she believe-

"The elegancies of life? The *elegancies*? Do you think I'm some stupid vapid fashionable idiot? Selling my soul for a few fripperies?"

"Of course not-"

"Really? Because that's what it sounded like to me!"

She stood glaring at him, her hands on her hips. Angry and magnificent.

"You're so beautiful." The words came without thought, right from his heart. "So wonderful. You deserve so much better than Muffet. I thought, if you were prepared to marry him, you might…" He was saying this all wrong. Wiping sweaty palms on his breeches, he took breath to try again, but she stopped him with a raised hand.

"Petroc Trengrouse, are you trying to *save* me? Is that what this is? You can't fight for your country any more, so you'll be the hero this way?"

"No!"

She took a step towards him, and stared right into his eyes. "Then why are you offering for me? *Why?*"

This was it. The moment he risked everything. He'd never been afraid of risk before. What the hell was wrong with him? But it was easier to ride into the mouth of a French volley than tell her the truth.

"Because I love you."

Beatrice took a step back involuntarily. *Loved* her? She didn't believe it, no matter that he was looking at her like a marooned man watching his ship sail away.

"Love me? You've never so much as kissed my hand!"

His whole body was tense, like a horse before the jump. He took her hand in warm fingers, and raised it to his lips. But instead of kissing the back, he turned it over and kissed the palm. A tremor went all the way through her. Perhaps he felt it, because he raised his head, his dark eyes warm and inviting.

Leaning back against the table for balance, he pulled her towards him. She could resist.

But he said he loved her.

He pulled her until their bodies were close, pressed together, length to length. The heat from his thighs against hers. The strength in his arms as they slid around her.

It was just like her dream. Except that now, Petroc tilted her head up to his, and brought his lips down towards hers. Slowly. Giving her time to move away.

His breath slid over her cheek, and she shivered. Immediately, he stopped, his mouth a mere inch away. Tentatively, she reached up, sliding her hand into the hair at his nape, her breath coming faster.

His breath hitched too, and then his mouth found hers. Heat rushed out from his lips, and fire slid up her body to meet it. She gasped for air, and then kissed him again, while his hands pulled her tighter against him.

She'd never dreamed she could be so *hungry* for more.

He kissed her mouth, her temples, her shoulder, nuzzled her neck… "Oh!" she said in soft surprise.

"I'm sorry-"

"No, it's all right. I just-" Best to call a halt there, or she'd be dragging him down to the sofa under the window, and only God knew what would happen then…although she had a fair idea. "Perhaps, though, we should…um…"

He moved his hands out to the side, leaving it to her to step back. Of course, he couldn't move away easily. Not without his crutches. Why was it so hard to pull away? She took a step back.

She should sit down. Discuss things calmly. Yes. That's what a lady would do. But before that, there was something she had to say.

"I-" *Breathe!* "I love you. At least, I think this must be love. It *feels* like love, but I've never been in love before, so I don't really know, I just-"

He was laughing at her! Her cheeks were hot with shame and beneath her ribs was an empty hollow.

"Oh my darling," he said, still laughing. "It *must* be love if my calm Lady Beatrice can't put two words together!"

Relief swamped her as he reached for her again. She put her hands flat on his chest, stopping him from kissing her.

"You shouldn't laugh when a lady pro-fesses her regard for you."

"Ah, *there's* my Lady Beatrice. I love you no matter how you talk, you know."

There was no doubting the look in his eyes.

"And I love you no matter how many feet you have." She slapped him gently. "Your mother is right. You're a complete ninny to think any decent woman would care about your injury."

"Easy to say." He stroked a strand of hair back behind her ear. "But you deserve the very best man on the face of the Earth."

She smiled, triumphant. "Yes, I do. I deserve you."

The kiss went on for longer this time.

Petroc couldn't quite believe it. It seemed so *unlikely* that Beatrice could care for him as a *man*. But there was no mistaking the passion in her embrace. He felt as though he were flying—it was like hunting over fences, soar and leap and soar again.

For the first time, the memory of riding athletically didn't hurt him. So, he'd lost the ability to do some things.

He had more than enough to make up for it right here, in his arms.

Her mouth was as sweet as he'd dreamed it would be, and when her languid eyes opened, what he saw in them was love.

An hour later, having had all his hopes and plans poured out to her, Beatrice sat with Petroc in his father's study.

She couldn't help but be nervous. What she'd told Mr Muffet was true—the Earl *did* intend advantageous marriages for his children. Demelza had told her so. She had nothing to bring to the marriage but Semper House.

If Petroc went through with his plans, perhaps that would be enough.

Uncle Jory looked up from the brief Petroc had put together.

"This all looks reasonable." He pushed his gold-rimmed glasses further up his nose. "Where do I come in?"

"Well, first we want your blessing."

Uncle Jory waved his hand. "Your mother's been preparing me for this since the day you got here. I swear that woman has second sight. Naturally we're delighted."

Tension curled in her stomach. Truly?

"But-"

"My dear, you're the daughter of two of our oldest and dearest friends. How could we be anything other than delighted?"

The relief warmed her whole body.

"So," Uncle Jory went on, "what do you need from me? Why this meeting?"

"I want you to sell me Blackfoot's colt." Petroc's voice was firm, but she could read his face so well now, and he was tense. A small muscle next to his mouth twitched.

"Do you now? For this horse stud of yours?"

"Yes. I have enough capital, and Semper House has a fine barn with stallion stalls. The dowager has agreed to us living there with her, and I'm pretty sure we can buy the land adjoining—at the worst, lease it. Ruby and Blaze are good breeding stock, but having Smetanka and the Godolphin Barb's line bred in can only do us good."

Beatrice almost laughed. Her mother hadn't just agreed, she'd been delighted, as much by realising she no longer had to face parties for Beatrice's sake as genuine happiness for the two of them.

"And your aim?"

"To train good, solid hacks."

"Not hunters?"

Beatrice frowned at the older man. How could he? There was no way a one-legged man could hunt or jump; which meant he couldn't train horses to. Uncle Jory smiled at her without apology.

"Very funny, Papa." The pain in his voice was gone. That *ache* which came whenever he'd talked about the future. He was his own man again.

"I daresay Blackfoot's colt will make an excellent wedding present, then."

Beatrice jumped up and went around the desk to hug him; a thing she wouldn't have even *thought* of doing six weeks ago. Petroc wasn't the only one who'd changed.

Swain Cove didn't seem such a prison if

she had Petroc to share it with, and there would be trips to Newmarket, and London, perhaps even abroad to find new breeding stock.

The whole world was ahead of them.

As they walked out of Uncle Jory's office hand in hand, she said so to Petroc. There was no one in the hall, but she wasn't sure he cared anyway. He just pulled her against him, leaning a crutch against the wall so she could nestle closer.

"The whole world," he murmured, and kissed her once, and then twice.

"Three times for luck," she said, and threw her arms around his neck as though she wasn't a lady at all.

MORE FROM ELIZABETH LEYDIN

I hope you've enjoyed the first book in the Trengrouse Ball series. There are more–see below.

Sign up for Elizabeth's Substack blog, 'Corsets & Coaches', where she shares true-life Regency stories and tidbits, as well as news about her latest releases, or watch her "This Week in the Regency" videos on Youtube.

More Trengrouse Ball Sweet Regency Romances

The Trengrouse Ball books can all be read as stand-alones – the timelines overlap, but each story is separate.

The Youngest Son
Book 2 in the Trengrouse Ball series

A heart-warming, forced marriage friends-to-lovers romance.

When Ives Trengrouse hijacks his friend Den's coach after the Trengrouse Ball, he thinks it's no more than a prank. But Den isn't inside. Instead, it's his sister Katie, going home early with a migraine.

Compromised beyond saving, the two must marry immediately—and do so. Katie's dreams of a big London Season are gone. Ives can't go on his light-hearted, care-for-nothing way now he's a married man.

Neither of them wants to be in this marriage: can they turn childhood friendship into something deeper?

Second Chance at Christmas
Book 3 in the Trengrouse Ball series

A heart-warming second chance Christmas story.

Widowed, pregnant Lady Demelza Mandeville returns to her family home, Trengrouse Hall, after her husband's recent death, dreading meeting family friend, Sir Denzell Kelynack, who jilted her in her first Season.

Denzell looks forward to the meeting—he wants to know why Demelza had jilted him eight years ago. And what role did his needy, unstable mother play in that?

Finding out the truth, and finding a path to a new life, is complicated by Demelza's pregnancy. If the baby is a boy, she'll be bound to the Mandeville estates until he's an adult; if a girl, she's free to live her own life while a Mandeville cousin inherits the estate.

The Trengrouse Ball is a promise of things to come, but will the promise come true at Christmas?

The Baboon at the Ball
Book 4 in the Trengrouse Ball series

A forbidden love story with animal antics to upset the normal order of things! (Or, a Cinderella story with a difference…)

Val Muffet is a Cit—a rich, well-educated, beautifully-mannered man, but definitely *not* one of the *ton,* despite being invited to the Trengrouse Ball.

Lady Kerenza Trengrouse's family is amongst the great and the good of the land,

and she expects to marry a lord. An earl, at least!

What could bring these two to care about each other? Enter Genevieve, the lost, forlorn but definitely challenging baboon, given to the Muffets by the Prince Regent himself.

Genevieve is *not* invited to the ball, but she comes anyway, and life will never be the same again for Val or Kerenza!

My Earl, the Spy
Book 5 in the Trengrouse Ball series

An exciting ace romance with a twist of espionage!

Lady Melissa Trengrouse can't imagine being married to anyone but Charles Goddard, Earl of Westholm, for whom she decodes secret French dispatches.

Although she hates the idea of marriage or children, for Charles, Melissa would endure it all. They're perfect for each other: but when she proposes to him at the Trengrouse Ball, he refuses her without explanation.

Charles has his reasons. He hates hurting her, but it's a relief when he has to ride off on a secret mission for the Crown.

Melissa realises he's riding into a trap. Can she save him and discover his secret reasons for denying that he loved her all along?

A sweet Regency romance with an atypical couple!

The Lion and Miss Lamb
Book 6 in the Trengrouse Ball series

Sarah Lamb doesn't have a family; Endellion Trengrouse has never fit in with his.

Immediately attracted, the two have a brief flirtation at the Trengrouse Ball, which ends disastrously when Endellion—known as Lion—finds out the truth behind Sarah's birth. Sarah isn't surprised by his reaction: she knows no respectable man will marry an illegitimate orphan.

But there's more to Sarah's parentage—and Endellion's—than either of them know. Can they find the truth…and will that truth bring them together, or drive them apart?

This story first appeared in the Sweet Daughters of Duke Street series.

www.ingramcontent.com/pod-product-compliance
Lightning Source LLC
Chambersburg PA
CBHW071017180726
48291CB00004B/1507